The Rat Tree

Susan M. Carr

Illustrations by Lauren Iida

Also by Susan M. Carr:

The Ballad of Desiree

Lost My Voice

Born

The Carmen Miranda Show

Geisha

After So Many Years

M.O.M.

THE RAT TREE

The sun was blazing hot as I opened the side door of my mom's 1954 Buick station wagon. The heat of the summer sun beat down on my back as I took off my flip-flops, and my feet felt the coolness of Grandpa's lush green lawn. My little sisters, Kathy and Izzy, ran by me as quickly as they could, grabbing their beach towels and backpacks. Every summer all of our cousins gathered here for get-togethers.

"Beat you to the mill," Kathy challenged our youngest sister, Izzy, who fumbled with everything she could hold in her tiny arms.

I walked slowly towards the tree. It was a large tree, four times the size of me. Dead rats hung from it, yet I could barely see them hidden behind the leaves. In winter, the tree was a frightening vision. It grew near the entrance of an old two-story woolen mill that my grandfather owned. I had to pass by the rat tree to get to the mill.

A car honked and another station wagon full of kids arrived, but I stayed put and stared at the tree.

"Boo!" Cousin Carl stood right behind me.

"You know I don't scare easily," I said.

"Why do you think he has them hanging there all the time?" Cousin Carl tried to push me off my balance.

"Because they're innocent," I said.

"Innocent. Oh that's deep. I'm getting hot. Come in and get your swimsuit on." Cousin Carl tickled me and ran down the short path to the door of the woolen mill.

As I pushed open the door, the mill was very dark. Cobwebs hung from the brown walls. There was a lingering smell of cigar smoke. Sun shafts reflected tiny particles of dust floating in the air.

"Oh, you took too long." Cousin Carl threw his beach towel around me. "Aren't you glad to be out of school soon?"

"Yes, oh yes. Spending my summer vacation swimming every day at the pool is going to be the best vacation ever."

We started to twirl again, but Cousin Carl bumped into one of Grandpa's work tables. "Ouch."

"You okay, Cousin Carl?"

"What is all this junk?" Cousin Carl picked up a hammer and hit the head of it on the table.

Hammers of many sizes hung on nails. Also chisels, saws, anything that a handyman might need. There were skill saws, drills, axes, pipes, screwdrivers, sanding machines, cutting machines, welding gloves and goggles. In a corner there was an old potbelly stove and above the stove were pictures. Naked women on calendars. Old photos of people I didn't recognize. Maps of 1930's Europe and more pin-up pictures of girls from the 1940's.

I pointed to Miss October. "Who is that, Cousin Carl?"

"That's Betty Grable. Come on and go change. I'm out of here." Cousin Carl turned quickly and slammed the door behind him, shaking rows and rows of cans on the shelves. Coffee cans, tomato paste cans, cut bean cans, cream corn cans, about every imaginable can that I would see on a grocery shelf. These cans held my grandfather's treasures: nickel-color nails, screws, bolts, grease, coins, and dead spiders. The Havana cigars had their own special hiding place, a beautiful thin box painted with lyrical writing and an exotic woman on it.

In the back of the woolen mill, Grandpa had concocted two changing rooms. There were no signs on the doors. No girl or boy symbols. The dark brown plywood swinging doors had an opening on the top and bottom so you could see people's feet and the tops of their heads. There was a golden latch inside to make sure that no one could come in. As I opened up the latch to go out, I heard something scampering on the floor. "Anybody there?"

Right in the middle of the main floor, a puff of dust stirred up. I looked up at the stairs leading to the second floor, across the changing rooms to the bathroom. The bathroom had an old toilet and an old sink with an old feeling to it. I touched the handrail and almost placed my foot on the thirty steps that took me up into darkness.

Izzy opened the door to let the sunshine in. "Are you coming or not? We're waiting for you in the pool."

"I'm coming." I yanked my flowery bathing cap on. "Race you to the pool."

*****

Izzy ran as fast as she could through the swinging door to the pool. Grandpa had a sign stating, "You must take a shower." Behind the swinging door was the open outdoor shower.

I skirted along the ten-foot-wide concrete sidewalk that surrounded the pool. There was a deep end with a diving board and a shallow end with a plastic white and pink rope separating them. Blue, orange, and black Italian mosaic tiles surrounded the sides of the pool. A six-foot red-cedar fence enclosed the pool. I waded into the deep end and floated on my back, staring up at the cloudless sky. It was heaven to have a pool where I could stay all day and late into the evening on a hot summer day.

*****

I dried off and placed my flowery bathing cap on my lounging chair.

Aunt Sissy was giggling. She paraded around in her new bathing suit. "Now what was it that you said to me, my little Carl?" She pushed Cousin Carl's head into her voluptuous bosoms.

"Oh Ma. You look beautiful." Cousin Carl pulled away and stared up at his mother's eyes.

"Grandpa, isn't he the sweetest boy a mother could ever have?" Aunt Sissy twirled Cousin Carl over to Grandpa Scheibert.

Aunt Diane, the youngest of the six daughters, sat down on Grandpa Scheibert's lap and poked at him. "If there isn't a Budweiser in your hand, then there is a shot of whiskey." She tried to take a sip of his whiskey.

"Sissy, you're making him a mama's boy." Grandpa's square jaw chomped down on his cigar. Aunt Diane and Sissy laughed away as Cousin Carl saw his father, Uncle Lou, arriving in the driveway. "Just look at your husband." Grandpa Scheibert took a swig of his drink.

"Oh Grandpa." Aunt Sissy sashayed in front of Grandpa and walked over to her husband, Uncle Lou. Uncle Lou kneeled down and hugged Cousin Carl. He flashed a smile at his adoring wife. He towered over both of them like a gentle giant. His funny smile reminded me of my dog, Snivels. All three of them walked up the pathway arm in arm, and Uncle Lou nodded to Grandpa.

Grandpa Scheibert sat under his covered porch on a barn-red lounge chair. His dark eyes peered out through his black aviator glasses. Grandpa's smile never appeared loving like Uncle Lou's. His was devious, disturbing.

*****

Cousin Carl opened the window on the east side of the mill. "Hey you, come into the mill. I want to show you something."

I looked up from my sandals and ran to the mill.

"Come play hide and seek with me," Cousin Carl called from the changing room.

"Sure."

Cousin Carl began to count. "1, 2, 3, 4, 5."

I found a spot underneath an old rug that had been thrown across some broken chairs.

"I can hear you." Cousin Carl crept slowly up the second-floor steps.

I also heard a noise as I watched Cousin Carl through a small hole in the rug. The noise couldn't be from me because I was totally still. Above both of us something moved across the floor. Cousin Carl stopped at the third step.

"Oh, you're too good. I give up. I can't find you." He backed down off the stairs.

"I can tell you if you're hot or cold." I moaned like a ghost underneath the rug.

Cousin Carl turned his head directly to where I was hiding.

Just then the door opened and Cousin Carl ran towards my peeping eye-hole. I pressed my lips hard against my hand, sealing in any audible breath. Cousin Carl crouched down low beside me.

Our younger cousins, Jimmy and Cousin Carl's brother, Little Lou, tiptoed by us. "I think they are hiding over there," Jimmy whispered to Lou.

"Let's scare them." Cousin Carl's words brushed by my ear. I looked up at his brown eyes and nodded. Cousin Carl and I leapt out behind Jimmy.

"Boo!" we hollered.

"Ahhhhh! Let's get out of here. There are ghosts here." Jimmy and Little Lou dashed to the front door and slammed it.

Cousin Carl and I fell down on the wooden floor planks and laughed our heads off. "Cousin Carl, do you ever wonder where Grandpa came from?" I asked, looking up at all the maps on the dingy walls.

"Someplace in Austria, Hungary."

"Where is that?" I asked.

Cousin Carl took my hand and walked me over to a faded map

of Europe and pointed to a small country on it. "There, somewhere."

I squinted at the tiny spot on the map and wondered why I had never heard of it. I had seen maps of Europe in my school, but I didn't recognize that name. "What is that writing, there on the corner?" I pointed to a dingy yellow border of the map.

"It looks like a word...Fatherland." Cousin Carl squinted at the scribbled word.

"What is Fatherland?" I said. "Do you know anything about Grandpa, Cousin Carl?"

"My mom says that he came over here with his brother."

"Where are his mother and father?"

"Aunt Alice says his mother was a mean German. No one ever talks about his dad. Why do you ask?" Cousin Carl and I dusted ourselves off as we walked over to the window.

"He's always watching everyone behind those big sun glasses. He seems mean to everyone. I just wonder why." We both looked out to the swimming pool filled with all our cousins splashing and shouting.

"I could find out more about where he came from, from my history teacher. She knows a lot about that stuff."

*****

The house that Grandpa Scheibert built was a pebble house. Rocks of different shapes and colors bulged out of the cement that bonded them. Even though there was a front door, no one ever used it. Izzy and I entered through the side door. When the screen door opened, there were stairs to the left leading down to a wood paneled basement.

Stairs to the right led up to a white kitchen where Grandma's stainless tea pot regularly whistled its tune on her kitchen stove so that everyone could sit and have a cup of Irish tea. "Are my two favorite grandgirls here?" Standing only four foot, eight inches in her stocking feet, she scooted over to her white enameled stove, turning off the kettle. "We've got some special cookies in the cookie jar," she sang as she opened up her kitchen cabinets to find some tea bags. Grandma had a large ceramic jar with cookies painted on it. We lifted the lid and grabbed Thumbprint cookies with raspberry jam, M & M cookies, and chewy toffee squares. No wonder Grandma was broad in the hips and shoulders. Sitting low in her chair, Grandma giggled at her feet that never touched the ground.

"Grandma, can I wear a muumuu like you?" Izzy politely sipped her tea.

"Oh you've got to go to Hawaii first," Grandma said.

"Does Hawaii look like your muumuu?" I admired the colorful tropical patterns on her dress.

"Oh yes it does, but you have to learn to dance there too." A Hawaiian singer, Don Ho, began to sing "Tiny Bubbles" on Grandma's radio in the corner. Grandma took our hands, lifted us up, and we swayed side to side, mimicking Grandma's hips gyrating and her arms waving. Grandma's radio was her constant companion when Grandpa went out to the woolen mill. "Now you two run up to the attic and play while I clean up." Grandma gathered her porcelain cups and saucers and began hand washing them at her sink.

Leaving Grandma's perfect kitchen and her classic Hawaiian songs, Izzy and I wandered through the narrow hallway of Persian rugs and then up the stairs. Upstairs was where all the sisters had lived, two large rooms for Dobbie, Diane, Alice, Linda, Sissy and our mother, Franny. In the pink room, there were three beautiful vanity sets with chiffon curtains that flowed to the floor.

"Let's go in and be princesses," Izzy begged. Izzy picked up a small hand mirror from her favorite vanity set. "It is so beautiful." She touched the silver pearl-handled mirror and matching brush. I liked the set with oval and square glass perfumed bottles.

"I know, I know. Let me spray some perfume on you," I said. We sat next to each other and stared at the mirror etched with a braid of flowers on the top edge.

"Will you brush my hair?" Izzy placed the brush in my hand. I braided her hair as she spritzed sweet smelling perfume under my ears and on my wrists. "Too bad you don't have long red hair like me." Izzy touched her soft, beautiful red curls that fell past her shoulders.

I looked in the mirror at my mousey-brown hair.

"Someday when I get older, I will have long, beautiful hair just like you, my sweet sister."

We brushed the curtains aside and looked out the window.

"Look at the aunts below," I pointed as we heard Aunt Alice, the oldest, her voice chuckling. "You can always recognize her."

"Yes. Her voice is like a chicken," Izzy winked. "There's Aunt Linda and Uncle Rodger."

"He's wearing his cop's uniform. He must have just gotten out of work."

"Izzy and Susie, where are you?" our mother, Franny, shouted from the pool below.

We leaned out the top floor window. "Up here, Ma!"

Our mother was the most beautiful of the daughters, with coal black hair and beguiling brown eyes. Many said that she was a natural beauty like Elizabeth Taylor. Our dad, Patrick, an Irish outsider, handed her a tumbler of whiskey.

"There's a party going on downstairs. Let's go there." Izzy wiggled away from the window and danced out of the room. The noise and energy level of the adults soared. I passed through the kitchen. Grandma was nowhere to be seen. The stairs were steep and wide, so I grabbed the handrail.

The lights were low, but through the dimness I could see the smoke lingering like dense fog as Joe, the Italian uncle, quietly sat in the corner of the bar. Aunt Alice, his wife, talked with her high pitched

voice at Aunt Linda, who could have been my mother's twin.

Aunt Dobbie walked in with her husband, Denny, who was carrying a case of Schlitz beer. "Now Denny, make sure you show my dad some respect. Don't drink all those beers yourself. Offer him one," Aunt Dobbie bossed him.

"Oh quit nagging me," Denny said.

Aunt Dobbie made a Lucille Ball face and shushed him.

Grandpa's large bar glistened with many colorful bottles of alcohol. Brown bottles with names like Jameson Whiskey, Corby's Whiskey, Old Fitzgerald, Seagram's 7, and Canadian Club. Gordon's Gin, Beefeaters, and Tanqueray London Dry were some of the clear glass bottles.

"Oh, I just love that record..." Aunt Linda mumbled to Aunt Diane. "I love 'Run Around Sue.'"

"Let's go dance," Aunt Diane said, pulling Aunt Linda off her stool. They moved their arms, hips and feet on Grandpa's huge dance floor. Camel cigarettes dangled from their mouths as they shook their heads. The songs became more upbeat and everyone screamed. Grandpa smoked his Cuban cigar and pounded the wooden bar counter.

When Franny and her best friend, Riet, entered, they held each other upright. Grandpa watched Riet. She was from Sweden. A strand of yellow, pale hair had fallen from the tight French twist that flattered her pale skin and eyes. My mother pinned Riet's fallen strand into place, and her eyes caught Grandpa's eyes. She took a long puff on her Camel and blew the smoke in his face. Grandpa rolled his cigar in his hand and chuckled under his breath. My mother grabbed my hand and pushed me back to the kitchen stairs. "Do you think I look fat?" She was pressing her hand on her stomach. "Riet is so beautiful and so slender, don't you think?"

Before I could answer, Riet shouted over to my mother, "Get back in here and buy me a martini."

Grandpa pulled down his silver metal mixer. He pointed to a gin bottle.

"Dad, you know what she wants." My mother pulled another cigarette from her purse and gave one to Riet. They both sat down together, flirting and making Grandpa happy.

As the next song played, Grandpa followed my mother and

Riet onto the dance floor. Grandpa pulled Riet close to him. He slid his hand down onto her rear end and leaned his mouth to her ear. A sly grin came across his face as he pressed his chest closer to her breasts. Grandpa was like a fox dancing with her. His ability to throw a quick feel on her neck, her chest, her rear was a dance in itself. My mother and I watched him closely, as all the others danced in a fog of booze and cigarettes.

Something inside of me began to burn. I moved towards Riet. I placed my body like a rock just behind Grandpa's back legs. To my surprise he started to stumble. "What was that?" Grandpa caught himself from faltering to the ground. My height and quickness made me invisible and totally unnoticed. How can he think that he could get away with that behavior? This man who was supposed to be a father, a Grandfather, and a husband. How could he do this to Grandma? Camouflaged behind Grandpa's leather cowboy couch, I looked around the room and realized that she wasn't there. I scooted out of the room and towards the furnace room looking for her. Clothes hung from lines crisscrossed above my head with hundreds of brown wooden clothes pins. The floor was smooth, dark grey concrete and on one side were her washer and dryer and a utility sink. The furnace in the back of the room loomed like a large oak tree. Grandma was taking out bottles of beer from her refrigerator again.

"Hey Grandma! Are you having a good time?"

"Oh yes, my little pumpkin eater. You want to help me carry these beers over to Grandpa?"

"Anything to help you, Grandma."

"Be careful and hurry up there."

"Yes, yes," I said. Uncle Lou saw me right away and helped grab the bottles that were moving in opposite directions in my folded arms.

"Now, now, let me help you, cousin."

"Thank you, Uncle Lou." Uncle Lou was the giant of the family, the one right out of Jack and the Beanstalk. He towered over me at 6' 7". Broad shoulders, big hands, and a round face. "Where is Grandpa Scheibert?"

"Over in the back corner." Uncle Lou pointed.

"What are they doing over there, Uncle Lou?"

"They're playing craps."

"What's that?"

"A dice game."

"Dice. I can throw dices."

"Yes, I bet you can, but they're betting with money and using bad language. And that isn't what you need to hear. Run along and find Carl. I know you like to play hide and seek with the rest of the kids. Why don't you get a game going?" Uncle Lou patted my shoulder and guided me away from the party.

*****

It was another beautiful day. Izzy, Kathy and I were beaming ear to ear as we opened the car door and jumped out with our new sundresses on. I loved that our dresses were all alike with special strings that tied up on our shoulders. Mine was pink. Kathy's was yellow and Izzy's was pale blue. We skedaddled up the driveway looking for Grandma who was sitting with Grandpa in their lounge chairs.

Skipping up, all three of us hugged Grandma's legs as she greeted us.

"Oh my sweet things!" She bent down to hug us back. "Give Grandpa a hug too."

Grandpa was lying on his chair being very still. Izzy jumped up into his arms and chest as Cathy sat on his legs and then reaching out with one arm, Grandpa placed his hand under my dress and touched my underpants. His fingers pressed onto my private area, feeling me hard up inside. I pushed him away and slapped his hand.

"Ugh!" A primitive sound came out of my mouth. I clenched my teeth and my eyes teared up. "Run from Grandpa!" I pushed Kathy off her balance. Immediately, Izzy started kicking Grandpa. I reached for her hand, and we both started yelling, "Run from Grandpa."

"Karl, look what you did. Scaring the little ones," Grandma said.

I made sure that he wasn't following us. We all bumped into mother's legs.

"Now settle down, girls, for your own good, or Grandpa will come after you," said my mother.

Grandpa grabbed Grandma and pulled her back towards him.

"Do as I say." Mother pushed us towards the woolen mill. "Get your suits on."

*****

I signaled to Izzy and Kathy to hurry and then slammed the door behind us and scanned to see if anyone was in the mill. "Let's all get our swimsuits on together in the changing room." I breathed deeply and settled down.

"Can we play that game again?" Izzy asked.

"What game?" I opened the swinging plywood door.

"The one we just played, Run from Grandpa," Izzy yelled at the top of her lungs.

"No! I have a better game." I removed my clothes and stood naked in front of them. "If Grandpa touches you here…" I put my hand on my breasts, and then I cupped my hand on my vagina. "If Grandpa touches you here, you are to yell as loud as you can, RUN FROM GRANDPA."

Kathy and Izzy were startled. I could see it in their eyes, but they only could see that my eyes were filling with tears.

"What's wrong? You are making us feel like there is something wrong," Kathy spoke up.

"There is something wrong. Grandpa is not to be trusted. He is a mean man, and I know that the only way to protect ourselves against him is to stay together, all three of us. Not any of us should be alone with him. Do you understand?" My voice was intense and loud.

"Yes, yes we understand." Kathy and Izzy surrounded me and held me like a big blanket.

Tiny eyes peeked through the holes in the changing room.

"Now let's finish putting our suits on and go to the pool," I whispered into their ears. Slowly the tiny eyes vanished one by one.

*****

Cousin Carl and I sat under the filbert trees, staring up at the thick canopy of leaves. "Not much grass underneath these trees," Cousin Carl said.

"A few nuts are beginning to fall." I picked up a hazelnut and felt its prickly cover. "Cousin Carl, do you ever notice anything strange about Grandpa Scheibert?"

"Other than he smokes cigars and drinks beer and pinches all of his daughters and Grandma too?"

"Well, do you think that he is strange when he pinches them? Does he pinch you, Cousin Carl?"

"No. Grandpa only roughhouses with the boys." Cousin Carl drew circles in the dirt with a fallen branch.

"He roughhouses with the young boys but not the uncles." I circled my finger in the dirt.

"Oh yeah. He usually wants to start a fight with the uncles and then they want to slug it out with him." Cousin Carl handed me a stick.

"I know. Remember last Thanksgiving? My mom was pretty drunk, and my dad wanted to leave."

"Yeah and then what happened?" Cousin Carl hit my stick.

"Grandpa Scheibert just kept grinning and taunting him by saying, 'Let her be,' to my dad's face. Grandpa's face seemed like he had a joker face on, a mean joker face. My dad started to raise his fist, but Grandpa just turned away. Are you scared of Grandpa Scheibert?" I hit his stick.

He hit it back. "I'm not scared of anyone." Cousin Carl picked up a nut and put it in his pocket. "Are you scared of Grandpa?"

My eyes welled up with tears. "Yes I am. He just did a bad thing to me."

"What did he do?" Cousin Carl snapped his stick in half.

"My sisters, Izzy, Kathy and I went over to sit on his lap. I stood there in front of him, and he touched me under my sundress. He touched my private place."

"Oh sweet cousin, what did you do?" Cousin Carl's face turned pale.

"We ran away from him as fast as we could."

"That son of a bitch!" Cousin Carl jumped to his feet and

kicked the tree trunk.

"Don't hurt yourself." I jumped up and put my hands on his shoulders.

"We've got to stop him." Cousin Carl looked at me.

"I know, but I need for you to look at something in the mill with me."

*****

"Can you see any light coming through here?" Cousin Carl knocked on the changing room's door.

"Yes, I can see the light from your flashlight, Cousin Carl."

"Really? You can see it?" Cousin Carl came around into the changing room.

"It's right here," I pointed to several small slits between the wooden panels, large enough for a tiny or even bigger eye to see through.

"Do you think he does look at us?" Cousin Carl asked.

"I don't know about you, but I get a creepy feeling every time I'm in here. I'm going to start dressing with a towel around me. It's that creepy."

Cousin Carl took my hand and led me out of the changing room to a big window by the bathroom. We unhinged the window lock and lifted it and breathed in the fresh air of the night. In the main house, we heard the aunts and uncles screaming loudly with a drunken bravado. Cousin Carl looked up at the moon. "There she is!" A sliver of a moon shone over the tiny lit-up houses.

"Cousin Carl, what should we do?"

"I don't know."

"Should we tell anyone?"

"We'd just get in trouble."

"You're right. We're just kids."

"Let's make a pact." I extended my hand.

"What are you going to do? Cut me?"

"No. Let's hold hands really tight and vow to watch over each other."

Cousin Carl took my other hand and squeezed it. "I, Cousin Carl vow to protect you from Grandpa Scheibert."

We opened our eyes and quickly let go of each other's hands. In the background we heard our names being called. "I guess we better get back."

"Yes, I guess we should." Cousin Carl led me over to the mill's front door. He turned around and put his hand on my shoulder. "You're a brave girl!"

*****

The next day Cousin Carl and I went for a walk behind the old mill.

"Did you find out anything?" I asked.

"My teacher, Sister Beasley said that Fatherland is connected to Germany and Hitler."

I stopped for a moment and sat down underneath one of the old filbert trees. "Some of my friends are Jewish, you know. When you put Hitler and Germany in one phrase, it is never a good thing."

"I know, I know." Cousin Carl looked at me with empathic eyes. "Go on."

"Well, you know how Grandpa always says that he is from Austria Hungary. That's not correct. It is Austro-Hungary. Austro-Hungary means that Hungary and Germany were friends in the war. Hungary supported Germany. That country was against the Jews."

"Wow. When did Grandpa come to the United States? I always thought it was when he was six years old."

"I'm not sure," Cousin Carl answered. "I think we should ask him some more questions and figure this out."

"We could say that we're finishing up a school project and need to interview him for it," I said.

"Good thinking."

I dusted the dirt from my shorts and looked up at the clear blue sky. "But first we have to go swimming. You never know when it might rain."

"Since I changed already, I'll meet you at the pool," Cousin Carl said.

"Wait. Would you mind coming with me?"

"Sure, anything to make you feel better."

"Grandpa, are you in here?" Cousin Carl imitated Grandpa's voice.

I laughed as we passed by all of Grandpa's works of art. I noticed my swim suit, towel, swim cap and goggles were on the stairs going to the second floor. The stairs were quite wide, not normally like stairs going up to an attic. They were rough cut, twenty thick plates of wood, stained with oil and dust.

"Did you do that?" Cousin Carl asked.

"No, I didn't. Everything looks like it was dragged up there." I started to crawl up each step to pick up my stuff. Cousin Carl was right next to me. We were silently making eye contact. About halfway up, I stopped. Ahead of us was an opening to the top floor, but it was very dark. The air smelled dank, and strands of cobwebs hung from the rafters. "What do you think is up there?" I asked.

"What I can barely see are old trunks."

"Trunks, huh? I wonder what's in them."

"I'm a little too scared to see what might pop out." Cousin Carl flailed his arms like a ghost.

"Don't do that!"

"See. You're just as scared as me."

"Yes. But maybe two people scared could be better than one. Don't you want to see what's in them?"

"Maybe after lunch." He smiled.

*****

During lunch, I became increasingly aware of everything and everyone. The colors of the gingham table cloth on the picnic tables, the plastic cups with happy bears dancing, Grandma running back and forth to her kitchen bringing out large trays with watermelons painted on them, mounds and mounds of peanut butter and raspberry jam sandwiches. Grandma knew I was different. She brought me peanut butter and jam wrapped in iceberg lettuce, whole milk and a big kiss on my cheek.

Most of the aunties were fussing over Grandpa. Getting him a sandwich. Getting him a beer. There was no need for him to ever get up. He lounged in his chair, wearing the old wife beater that Auntie Diane always talked about. Most of his clothes were from Sears or JC Penny's. Blue Levis with a black leather belt. Of all the smokers in the family, he was the only one who smoked a cigar, rolling it over and over between his thumb and second finger. The wooden match crackled with fire as he drew his first puff of smoke. He waited an extra minute before he exhaled. His eyes looked intoxicated as he leaned back. A wicked smile crept across his face.

I quickly looked over to Cousin Carl to see if he had finished eating. "Let's open the trunks," I whispered.

"You go and I'll follow." He shoved some potato chips into his mouth.

I took my paper plate and cup over to the garbage bag. Walking by the rat tree, I noticed a new rat hanging. It wasn't very big like the others. More like a baby rat. My heart went out to it. "I'm sorry, baby rat, that he had to get you." I repeated it as a prayer.

Cousin Carl slapped me on my back. "Okay, let's do this."

*****

Now one of my towels was lying near the middle of the stairs of the woolen mill. "What's going on?" I went to pick it up but noticed my socks were farther up. "How did this get all the way up here?" I was mad as I stomped up to the top stair.

"Wait a minute." Cousin Carl ran up behind me with a headlamp. "Wear this."

"Thanks." I put on the headlamp and started to examine the upper room. Old frames dangled off the rafters. In the center of the room were trunks and wooden chairs with missing seats.

"See. Here it is." Cousin Carl's headlamp illuminated the biggest trunk. It had metal sides and a latch that looked like it was opened. There was no lock. "On the count of three, help me lift the top," Cousin Carl said.

"One, two, three." I used my upper body strength and presto, we lifted it up. "Wow, look inside." The top part of the lid inside had old pictures of people attached to it. They were marked with names and dates. Karl Scheibert, Maria Fuchs, 1904.

"I wonder if this was his mother and father." Cousin Carl rummaged through the pictures.

"Yeah, could be." There were also envelopes, addressed to Karl Scheibert, Milwaukie, Oregon. The returned address was Austria-Hungary. "Austria-Hungary!" I shook the letters.

Cousin Carl reached his hands through the piles of envelopes, shuffling them around until he saw a black book. He opened it, and we saw drawings of a young person with a house, a young person with dog, a young person with a mother. No father. Just the mother. The mother wore very old clothing, a long black skirt and a buttoned-up black blouse with a black shawl over her shoulders. Her hair was black and long. Her face was strange looking. Contorted. Her mouth was bigger than a normal mouth. Her teeth looked like fangs. The pictures continued with different ages marking them: six years, nine years, thirteen years, fifteen years, eighteen years and twenty years old. The twenty-years-old picture had a woman dressed in white with a veil on. Her face was contorted like the others. An exaggerated mouth with fanged teeth.

"She looks mean."

"Yes, she does," Cousin Carl said.

On some pages there was writing: *She stands there every day, looking down at me, just before breakfast. My cereal is getting cold, but she doesn't care. She looks at my hair, my clothes, my skin, and my fingernails. Every part of me has to be cleaned and in order. If she finds one thing out of place, she slaps my hands. Today was a good day. I can eat my cereal before it cools down.*

"I think he is writing about his mother," I said.

Today wasn't a good day. She makes me do the same thing over and over again. I have to clean the outhouse. She gives me a brush and a bucket full of water, and I scrub it inside and out. I don't like this job. She inspects it and tells me to do it over again. I do it again, but each time she inspects it, she slaps my hands. They are wet and red and sore from the lye soap, and her face is always sneering at me. I hate her.

"I think this is his diary," Cousin Carl said.

"You're absolutely right."

"His English is pretty good."

"What?"

"Grandpa said that his school taught English and German early on. The way he describes her. She sounds like a horrible mother to have," Cousin Carl said.

"No wonder he's a mean man," I said. I opened one of the envelopes and unfolded a letter. The paper was yellow and dried out, not like white new paper.

> *Karl,*
>
> *I write to you in English since you have forgotten your homeland. I am glad you are gone from me. No mother would want a son like you. You were never good enough. You and your father were not the kind of men that could be part of our Fatherland.*

"Fatherland. Just like my teacher said," Cousin Carl stated.

"We've been up here a little too long. Someone might come in looking for us. We'd better put away everything like we found it." I lifted the envelopes and replaced the book. I shuffled the letters so they were in even piles. Then I closed the lid.

The adults were yelling out our cousins' names, "Louanne, Carl, Timothy, Debbie, Tom...Time to go home."

I heard another sound. I looked behind me and saw little tiny eyes blinking all around the trunk.

*****

A few days later, I stared at Cousin Carl's very white cast.

"What happened to you?"

"Football. I jammed my ankle when I fell." The gentle giant wobbled on his crutches.

"Hobble over to the patio and I'll get you a Coke."

Mary, Janet, and Jimmy were jumping off the diving board into the refreshing pool. Cousins Tom, Little Lou, and Louanne squealed at the top of their lungs in the shallow end when Grandpa Scheibert entered the pool.

"The kids sound frightened." Cousin Carl tried to lift himself up on his crutches.

"I just got my birthday goggles. I'll go check them out." I dove into the deep-end to see clearly what Grandpa Scheibert was doing. He was pulling the boys' pants down even though the little kids were kicking at him. I hoisted myself out of the pool.

Cousin Carl was pacing back and forth on his crutches underneath the patio when he saw me. He hobbled over toward the swinging door of the pool. "What is he doing?" Cousin Carl asked.

"You know, the usual."

"Louanne sounds scared." Cousin Carl tried to look around me.

"I'll go back in and play with her." Cousin Carl turned away from me, but as I spun around I found Grandpa Scheibert right in front of me. His towel was wrapped around his waist. I jumped out of his way.

"Feeling any better, Carl?" Grandpa Scheibert wrapped his big arm around Cousin Carl's neck and locked it tight. Cousin Carl was doing a great job of balancing on one foot as I took one of his crutches and started jabbing Grandpa with it.

"We got you out of the pool, didn't we Grandpa?" I teased him.

All the little cousins ran up behind Grandpa and started to push on him. He let go of Cousin Carl. Then they dashed as fast as they could back to the mill. Grandpa laughed as Cousin Carl and I joined them. Cousin Carl closed the door as soon as we were all in the mill. "Ok, we need all of you to pledge something to Cousin Carl and me." Nine tiny faces looked up at us.

"From now on, we will protect you from Grandpa Scheibert,"

Cousin Carl said. "We are the adults." Cousin Carl pulled out a large white sketch book and charcoal pens from his pack and drew pictures of a young boy and a young girl. He carefully drew breasts on the girl and pubic hair and then just pubic hair on the boy. Everyone's eyes opened wide.

"We need you to tell us if anyone touches you here." I took my finger and touched the breasts and pubic hair on the girl. Cousin Carl touched the pubic hair on the boy. "If someone touches you any place, that is inappropriate," we said firmly.

"What does that mean?" Little Louanne said.

"It means that if someone older than you touches your breasts or where your hair is..." I realized that some of them didn't even have any hair there yet. "People older than you are not supposed to touch you even where you go pee. It is wrong. They cannot touch you, and you should not let them." Everyone turned their heads to each other as their mouths fell downwards.

"We are going to take a pledge. Repeat after us." Cousin Carl took over. Suddenly the little cousins raised their hands and placed them on their chest. Cousin Carl and I began the pledge. "I pledge that if anyone like Grandpa, or uncles or friends try to touch me in a wrong way, I will immediately slap, bite, scratch, kick at the person and come running to Cousin Carl or Cousin Susie." They all repeated the pledge.

*****

Aunt Dobbie, Aunt Alice, Aunt Diane, Aunt Sissy and Aunt Linda arrived with all of our cousins the following weekend. We had decided to do a play about Grandpa. The oldest of the cousins were me, Carl, and Karen, whom we had not yet asked to join us. The other cousins were too young to understand what we were about to do, but if we told them that we were going to put on a play then they would want to be part of it. Everyone wants to be in a play.

"Should we talk about what we are doing with Karen?" I asked Cousin Carl.

"No. I think if you and I know why we are doing this, then we will have the final say."

"Okay. How about after lunchtime? We could gather everyone together and tell them that we're going to ask Grandpa some questions. I'll go tell Grandma that we want to do this. I'll tell her that we want Grandpa to tell us a story about his childhood."

"Good idea." Cousin Carl waved at his mother.

"Carl, get all the cousins together and assign which ones should ask the questions." Cousin Carl motioned to the cousins, and they filed into the mill one by one to change into their swimsuits.

I opened the screen door and called out, "Grandma!" Grandma was listening to her radio and hand washing her dishes. She had another flowery muumuu on, and this one had a huge pink and purple flower on a deep blue background. She was humming along with her favorite song, "Let Me Call You Sweetheart."

Let me call you Sweetheart, I'm in love with you.
Let me hear you whisper that you love me too...

I tugged on her dress. "What do you want, my sweetie?"

"After lunch, do you think Grandpa could sit with all of the cousins and talk about his childhood?"

"Well, I don't see why not? Come to think of it, I don't even know that much about Grandpa's past. He is sort of quiet about it."

"We would love to ask him questions for a school assignment."

"Well if it is for school, then we should do it. Could you help me make some sandwiches for the kids?" Making food with Grandma was one of my favorite things. She explained all about the ingredients for tuna sandwiches; sweet pickles, onions, celery and white tuna chopped up fine with lots of Best Foods mayonnaise. To begin she laid bread and butter pickles and iceberg lettuce on Franz white doughy bread. I laid out the bread slices, and she doled out one scoop of tuna mixture and firmly spread it down. I placed on the pickles and lettuce, and she put the top slice of bread down. Then she carefully cut the sandwiches into four triangles. I added some Lays potato chips to each plate. "You kids could have some cookies from the cookie jar while you are talking to Grandpa."

I glanced over at the big ceramic cookie jar that was always filled. I smiled back at her kindness to all of us but wondered about her and Grandpa.

Meanwhile, Cousin Carl had gathered all the cousins together in the mill. He had assigned Karen, Louanne, and Little Mikey each a question to ask Grandpa. Grandma and I set the plates and apple juice down on the long picnic tables underneath the outdoor patio. Grandpa was cleaning the pool out. He had his Cuban cigar lit and his sunglasses on. He seemed to be in a relaxed mood. "Mel, the pool is ready for the kids," he hollered to Grandma.

"We're having lunch first. Come over and sit with them." We ate, but there was very little talking going on. Grandpa wanted everyone to be well-behaved. He used to take any of the kids who weren't good over to where the rats hung upside down on the tree branches and warn us that we would be hanging there too if we didn't behave. "Honey, the kids have a school assignment. They want to ask you some questions about when you were a kid."

Grandpa looked up with a little bit of tuna on the side of his mouth. He chuckled. "Okay, who wants to ask me a question?"

Cousin Carl and I looked over to each other and raised our hands, but out of the blue, Little Mikey jumped in. "Where did you come from?"

"The alien," Grandpa responded with a gruff deep voice.

Oh no, is he thinking that this is a funny game with funny answers? I decided to break into the laughter. "Oh Grandpa, that is so funny, but our teacher won't find it funny. Where did you come from?"

"I told you Austria-Hungary," Grandpa snapped back.

"Do you mean Austro-Hungary?" Cousin Carl said.

Grandpa took out his cigar and slowly got up off his lounge chair. "Who told you about Austro-Hungary?"

Cousin Carl squeezed his apple juice carton so strongly it began to crush. "Oh, my teacher is telling us about the different countries during the war." My stomach had a bad ache in it.

"She's teaching you about the Nazis?" asked Grandpa.

I tried to keep my face relaxed and not react to that word, Nazis. "Grandpa," I interrupted, "maybe you can tell us about how you came over to America. Did you take a boat? Who came with you? How old were you?"

Grandpa puffed on his short stubby cigar. The ashes fell off the end of it. "I came with my father, my brother and my sister."

Good. My body relaxed as I pressed on. "What was your Dad like?"

"He was a blacksmith where we grew up. I was about twelve. I only had a sixth grade education."

"Did you go to school in America?" Cousin Karen asked next.

"No. I worked. We had to make money."

Little Mikey spoke up next. "I wish I didn't have to go to school."

The other cousins started talking over each other.

"What was your mother like?" Cousin Carl stopped the chatter.

Grandpa Scheibert took off his sunglasses and stared at Cousin Carl.

Grandma glanced at his piercing eyes. "Okay, everyone in the pool." Grandma began to clear the plates.

"Yeah, the pool!" The young cousins screamed.

Grandpa Scheibert stood up from his lounge chair and walked behind Cousin Carl and leaned slightly over him. Cousin Carl stayed perfectly still. "You better help your Grandma clean up if you know what is good for you."

I picked up a stack of plates and cups and dashed over to the main house. After I dried and put away the dishes, I hung my apron in the pantry closet. I brushed the white eyelet curtains aside to see if Cousin Carl was still sweeping up underneath the patio tables. Then I opened up the front door and looked both ways to see if Grandma or Grandpa were around. They were not. I walked outside towards Cousin Carl. Without saying anything, I nodded to signal to Cousin Carl to meet me at the mill.

When I entered the mill, I decided to walk up the stairs to where the trunk was. Suddenly, footsteps were coming up the stairs. My eyes had gotten used to the dark, and I could see Cousin Carl's silhouette. "Cousin Carl, that didn't go so well."

"Did you see the look that he gave me?"

"I didn't have to see it; I felt the hairs on my skin were standing straight up. We need to let him know."

"What do you mean?" Cousin Carl opened the trunk.

"If we take the letters and create a play about his life, then maybe he would change." I gathered the letters.

"Change....you mean....not be so mean?"

"Yes, maybe he would be different, less mean." I gave him a bunch of the letters. "We'll put on a play and invite Grandma, Grandpa, and all the aunts and uncles."

"We could do that."

We stared at all the letters. "Cousin Carl, you take some of the letters, read them and start to write ideas about what we want to say. Do you want to play Grandpa?" I gave one of the stick drawings to him.

"Just the thought of it bothers my stomach, but maybe I'll learn something about him."

"Great. Let's take the pictures that he drew and put them on us. Like re-create them on butcher paper," I said.

"Good idea."

"Some things we will have to make up. Maybe we will get a reaction or maybe we won't. He can't silence us anymore."

*****

I decided to be the director of the play about Grandpa. Everyone gathered upstairs in the attic of the mill. We had our miner head-lights on. The little cousins sat in a circle, forming the stage of the play. "Cousin Carl, you and Little Mikey hold hands together and walk across the room and pretend it is a street. Now Karen, you will be a soldier and stop them by stepping in front of them."

"Stop, you two!" Karen glanced over at me.

"Good, Karen, and say whatever comes to your mind."

"You there. Do you have a star on?" Cousin Karen pointed to Little Mikey.

Cousin Carl looked up from his feet. "But he is my friend. We are not doing anything wrong," Cousin Carl said.

"Now Karen, grab Little Mikey's arm," I said. Little Mikey moved. "No, Little Mikey. Stay there. You can't run away," I demanded.

"Cousin Karen is scaring me," Little Mikey confessed.

"Remember you are in a play, and she is just pretending. You pretend to stay still and keep your eyes on your feet," I told him.

"You need to put the star here," said Karen grabbing Little Mikey's arm.

"Yes sir," Cousin Carl said.

"Now," I continued, "all of you walk away. Good, everyone. Now the next scene. Louanne, you can play the mother, and Billy, you can play the father."

Cousin Louanne walked into the middle of the circle. Cousin Billy slowly got up but decided to sit down quickly. "Cousin Billy, are you okay?" I asked.

"I've never been in a play. I don't know what to do," he spoke slowly because Billy was a little slow.

"Well, we will help you."

"Okay, I will do it."

"Great. You and Louanne are going to fight. Cousin Billy, keep repeating this line, 'These people are good people.' Every time you feel like it, just say those words over and over. Cousin Louanne, has anyone ever been mean to you at school? Bullied you? Said mean things?" I asked.

"Yes." Her head light bobbed up and down.

"Now say to Cousin Billy, 'Cousin Carl's friend is a bad person. He is not like us. He needs to go away. Cousin Carl can never see him again.'"

"I hate you!" Cousin Billy yelled. Everyone gasped. "You are so mean," Cousin Billy said.

"Okay, Everyone. Let's take a break. We can work on this later."

*****

The cousins played happily on the hanging swing in the old maple tree, while others of them rolled around with each other on the nicely groomed grass. "They are really feeling the feelings," Cousin Carl said.

"Yes, I know. It is so powerful," I agreed.

"Do you think it's a mistake? Putting on this play?" Cousin Carl asked.

"I think you need to say the words in the diary about his friend. We won't have Louanne say the words because they might be too much for her. We'll draw the stick figures of Grandpa and his mother on butcher paper and then have the little cousins unrolling the paper while you recite your speech. Then they won't have to do too much. Go get Cousin Louanne and Billy."

When he returned with them I told them what we had decided. "Since both of you are such good drawers, we want you to draw these pictures and put them on big butcher paper. During the play, the little cousins will help un-roll them while you both stand and watch Cousin Carl. Would that work for both of you?"

"I love to draw," Cousin Billy said.

Cousin Carl gave them the drawings of a stick mother watching a little boy in a closet and a stick mother with a big mouth and sharp teeth looking at a very tiny boy with no shirt on.

"Louanne, make sure the ribs are very noticeable," I said.

*****

The weather was changing and fall was in the air. I wondered when the hazel nuts would fall off the tree.

"School starts soon." Cousin Carl shook a branch.

"Labor Day weekend is this weekend. All the grownups will be here."

"Let's do it this weekend," said Cousin Carl.

*****

It was another beautiful, hot weekend. Grandpa Scheibert rummaged through his many cans.

"Are you looking for something, Grandpa Scheibert?"

"You've been spending a lot of time in here with your Cousin Carl." Grandpa took out his cigar.

"Oh, oh yes," I chuckled. "Cousin Carl and I are teaching the kids some new hide and seek games. So are you looking for something, Grandpa?"

Ashes dropped from his cigar. I spotted two large rats by the cans behind Grandpa. "I think you better turn around, Grandpa," I said. The rats tipped over the cans and scurried off in opposite directions.

"The kids are waiting for me." I dashed past him, my heart racing, and slammed the door shut.

"You lousy rats," Grandpa shouted.

I was free. My feet felt the sunshine. Cousin Carl stood on the diving board, waving. I clutched my white towel to my chest.

Grandpa Scheibert was coming out of the mill. Grandma yelled something to him. He raised one of his hands and shook it. She went back to the refrigerator to stack more beers.

I threw my white towel on the lounge chair and jumped into the deep end of the pool. The water cushioned my feet. I stood with my head well above the depth of the water. The little cousins waved me down to the shallow end to play Marco Polo. "Okay, okay, Marco Polo. I will be Marco Polo," I said. I closed my eyes and yelled, "Marco!"

"Swim away from her!" Little Mikey squealed.

Cousin Louanne, Little Mikey, Billy, Cousin Janet, and Debbie shouted back, "Polo!"

I swam towards their voices. The shallow end was not that big. I swam like a dog paddling in the water, and then someone kicked me. I jumped out of the water. Someone tapped my shoulder. It was Cousin Carl. He was holding the long net that scoops up debris from the pool. I laughed and yelled back, "Polo."

The aroma of hamburgers on the grill made me hungry. Aunt Sissy laid out red and white plastic table covers, and Aunt Linda and Franny followed up with white paper plates, plastic spoons and napkins. Grandpa and Uncle Lou slapped perfectly squared yellow slices of cheese on every hamburger patty. White buns from Franz bakery were prepared with tomatoes, lettuce and mayo.

I gathered the cousins by the side of the pool. "After lunch, we are going to do the play. When you are finished, go to the mill and get your costumes on. We will all walk out together. Okay?" All the cousins excitedly nodded their heads.

*****

"Everyone! Lunch is served." Aunt Sissy opened the wooden gate to the swimming pool. There was a mad dash as the little cousins climbed up the side ladder of the pool and filed out, grabbing their towels and swimming caps. I laid on my back looking up at the sky as a cloud floated by.

"You coming?" Cousin Carl stepped in front of my sunshine.

"I could just stay here." I squinted my eyes.

"Yes, you could. But we both promised."

"Race you to the deep end." I dove down and glided underwater, pushing my body hard and strong with each breast stroke. I lifted myself up onto the warm concrete side of the pool.

"You're fast." Cousin Carl handed me my towel.

The sky had no clouds in it now.

*****

Cousin Carl helped me gather the butcher paper roll. "Remember the order. Cousin Carl and Little Mikey and Karen will be first. Then Louanne and Billy will be after them. Cousin Carl and I will unroll the butcher paper as Louanne and Billy have their fight. Then Louanne and Billy will help me unroll the stick figure paper while Cousin Carl does his speech. Remember not to rush. Go slowly. All the other cousins should sit in a semi-circle in front of us to cheer us on."

Grandma waddled over to the nicely trimmed lawn by the big oak tree with the swing. "Ladies and gentlemen. Our little ones are going to present us a play today. Everyone clap for them."

As we walked out, I watched my father trying to pull my mother to a chair. He was grabbing for her drink.

"Don't touch me. I'll walk over when I'm good and ready."

Grandma hushed my father to sit down as she stood next to my mother.

Holding Little Mikey's hand, Cousin Carl skipped across the center of the green grass. My mother also started skipping and laughing as she came towards Karen.

I stood up, but Karen put her hand right up to my mother. "Stop you two!" she shouted.

"Sit down, Franny!" Grandpa Scheibert bellowed.

Grandma raced over to my mother who turned around and began yelling at Grandpa. "You can't tell me what to do."

"Oh yes, I can," Grandpa said.

"Ladies and Gentlemen!" I shouted at the top of my lungs. "The play must go on."

The little cousins shushed Grandpa and my mother. Cousin Carl looked up as Little Mikey looked down.

"You do not have a star on," Karen said.

"He is my friend. We didn't do anything wrong," Cousin Carl said.

"You have to wear the star here."

"He will," Cousin Carl said.

Little Mikey looked up with the most amazing face of innocence.

Billy and Louanne positioned themselves in the middle of the lawn. "I do not understand you," Louanne said.

"These people…are…good. These people…are…good. These people…are…good. These people…are…good," Billy repeated.

Billy was getting louder with each phrase, and my mother chimed in, "These people aren't good, these people aren't good." Then she stopped and laughed uncontrollably.

"No, they are not good people. They are bad people. They need to be removed. They are not like us," Louanne yelled over her.

"Be quiet, Franny. We want to watch the play," Aunt Sissy said.

"That's right, I'm not like you," Billy said.

All the cousins shouted, "Yeah!" and clapped their hands wildly. Billy and Louanne left the center of the lawn as Cousin Carl sat in the swing. There was a long pause. Cousin Carl spoke, as we unrolled the butcher paper with Louanne and Billy's drawings.

"I had a childhood friend, Abram who was my best friend. He was Jewish. When the Nazis started to warn my mother and father about being friends with the Jews, my mother told me that I couldn't see Abram anymore. She said that he was a bad child and needed to be removed by the Germans. Removed meant that all Jews needed to be killed. I would hear my father and mother fighting about the Jews, and there was much hatred from my mother's mouth. My father didn't believe that Jewish people were bad. I tried to help Abram by giving him food. When my mother found out, she decided to torture me for it. She dressed me up with a Star of David on my coat and made me walk down the streets. I saw how people looked at me, and some spit or threw rocks. She locked me up in a closet and made me sit there for hours with no light, no food, and no books. At night when she gave me a bath, she poured only cold water on me. My ribs stuck out more each day. My face became like a skeleton. She laughed at me standing naked in front of her. "Little Jewish boy lover. You're not a man. You're an ape lover. You're not a real German. You make me sick. You are not my son."

"You make me sick!" My mother pointed at Grandpa. "You make me sick. YOU!"

Grandpa got up from his seat and pushed towards my mother, knocking down Aunt Diane and Dobbie.

"Little Jewish lover, you're not a man, you're an ape lover.

You're not my son," my mother mocked him.

Grandpa grabbed my mother's hair and slapped her across the face. "You ungrateful bitch!"

"Stop this now, you son of a bitch," my father said punching my grandfather in the arm as my mother dropped to the ground.

"I hate you. You hurt me so bad. I hate you. You touched me, your own daughter. You sick son of a bitch," my mother cried.

I ran towards Grandma shouting, "Grandma, make him stop. Make him stop hurting my mother. He hurt me too."

Grandma screamed, "All of you stop this minute. She turned to face me. "What did you say?"

"He hurt me too, Grandma. He touched me."

"Oh Karl, you hurt my girls." Grandma held me so close to her.

My father tackled Grandpa to the soft lawn and then stood up and kicked him.

"Stop it! All of you!" Grandma screamed. "Oh Karl, how could you?" Grandma held me even closer.

"He was hurt, but he hurt me too. I was only a child. He had sex with me," my mother cried out loud.

The air was sucked out of all of us.

"Oh Karl, oh Karl you didn't," Grandma wailed.

I pulled away and looked at all of them as if they were on a stage. I didn't know. I didn't know that what Cousin Carl and I had found would lead up to this moment. My body remained frozen for a while. Then feeling Cousin Carl's hand in mine, my eyes adjusted back to the reality of all of it. My mother sobbing. My grandmother sobbing. My eyes had no tears. I felt sick and sorry that the secrets were told.

A large rat watched from the woolen mill door.

THE RAT TREE

ACKNOWLEDGMENTS

Thank you to Lauren Iida, Ralph Levin, Carolyn Hall, Ann Tracy and all my friends and students who support me.

AUTHOR'S BIO

When not writing, Susan is an actress and singer having performed in New York, Los Angeles, and Seattle. Her film/TV credits include Mike Mill's The Architecture of Reassurance, Rob Devor's ZOO, Paul Sorvino's That Championship Season, Lynn Shelton's Laggies, The Practice and Gilmore Girls. Susan's plays and screenplays have been performed at Seattle Fringe Festival, Bumbershoot and New City's New Works Festival. She is also a vocal coach working with Grammy-nominated bands such as Macklemore, The Head & The Heart, Alice in Chains, Alien Ant Farm, Mastodon and The Presidents of the United States of America. *The Ballad of Desiree* was her first novel. Susan teaches The Art of Screaming!

ILLUSTRATOR'S BIO

Lauren Iida was born in Seattle and holds a BFA from Cornish College of the Arts (2014). She shares her time between Seattle and Cambodia where she leads art tours, writes and illustrates bilingual books for children and works in her cut paper studio, the 'mobile atelier.'

Iida has exhibited her work at ArtXchange Gallery, King Street Station, the Mayor's Gallery at Seattle City Hall, Shoreline City Hall, Twilight Gallery, Tacoma Spaceworks and Sculpture Northwest. She is an Artist Trust GAP Grant recipient and her work has been collected by the City of Seattle. Iida is the founder of 501(c)3 non-profit The Antipodes Collective which creates high quality learning materials for Cambodian children through worldwide artistic collaboration.

Much of Iida's work is influenced by Cambodia where she has lived for many years working on various non-profit and social entrepreneurship projects beginning in 2008. Other major influences include her family's Japanese American heritage and incarceration during WWII and her Pacific Northwest home.

Made in the USA
San Bernardino, CA
28 February 2018